Hang-Ups

The love child of an Austrian prince and a '60s top model, Candy Barr was educated at a convent in Surrey and a finishing school in Switzerland. At the age of fourteen she landed her first film role, in Luigi Fettucine's controversial musical, 'Night of the Living Zombies'. Although on the threshold of movie stardom, she sacrificed her film career to devote herself fully to the life of the jet-set novelist. She now lives in Bel Air, Gstaad and Monaco with three borzois and a bird of paradise.

Candy Barr claims her heroine and literary mentor to be the writer Caroline Bridgwood, whose novels *This Wicked Generation*, *The Dew of Heaven* and *Magnolia Gardens* are also published by Pan Books.

Candy Barr

Hang-ups

Pan Original
Pan Books London, Sydney and Auckland

All characters in this book are fictitious, and any resemblance to actual persons, living or dead, is purely coincidental

First published 1988 by Pan Books Ltd,
Cavaye Place, London SW10 9PG
9 8 7 6 5 4 3 2 1
© Caroline Bridgwood 1988
ISBN 0 330 30251 5
Printed and bound in Great Britain by Richard Clay Ltd, Bungay, Suffolk

To my sister
Elizabeth

One

Jay Cathcart adjusted his Ray-Bans against the glare of the bright June sunshine and switched on the ignition of his Twin-Cam Turbo-charged Intercooler convertible. He checked his Rolex. Five o'clock. It had been an average day. Four hours of using the telephone in the office where he worked, and three hours for lunch in the trendy Basmati Brasserie in Holland Park. Now it was time to go home and assess the evening's possibilities.

Jay roared into Redcliffe Gardens, and double-parked in a place which ensured that no other motorists could pass on either side, and that those cars already parked couldn't possibly get out. Once inside the flat, he surveyed his surroundings with satisfaction. A vast white space served as his drawing room, empty except for a large graphite-coloured sofa and a reading light in the shape of a Friesian cow. Ceramic figurines of Wonderwoman flew up the white walls like ducks; the stripped wooden floorboards were quite bare except for their layer of white gloss paint. Jay frowned at the lone Gauloises butt screwed vertically into the Art-Deco ashtray, then remembered. It was the cleaning lady's day off.

The red light was flashing on his answering machine. He tossed his grey snakeskin Organofax onto the floor and

1

pressed the 'PLAY' button. Then he stretched himself out on the sofa with his hands behind his head.

'CLICK. Hi Jay, Suze here . . . it's Thursday . . . don't know what you're doing tonight, but why don't you give me a call and maybe we can get together . . . Byeee!'

'CLICK. Jay darling, it's Davina. Listen, I've had a brilliant idea about what we could do tonight. Call me back, okay?'

'CLICK. Jay; returning your message; the one you left on my machine after you were out and I'd left a message asking you to call me back. Sorry you were out again . . . I'll try later, or you could try ringing me — ',

Jay switched the machine off and lifted the receiver out of Mickey Mouse's white-gloved hand.

'Suze, hi . . . Jay Cathcart here. What's going down?'

A sleepy voice on the other end mumbled. 'What?'

'That bad, huh?'

'Yeah . . . listen, what was I going to tell you? Oh yes, a load of us are meeting at my place and going on to eat at King Kong's. D'you want to come?'

'Sounds great, why not? What time's everyone going to be there?'

'Eight-ish.'

'Eight. Great. See you then.'

Jay laid down the receiver, then lifted it again.

'Davina, hi, Jay Cathcart here.'

'Jay, darling, how wonderful!'

'So — what's everyone doing this evening?'

'Well, I thought since the weather's so marvellous I'd ask a few people round and we'd have some Pimms and play croquet on the roof terrace. Rory's coming, and Hugo. D'you think you can make it?'

'Love to. What time?'

'About nine?'

'Nine? Great. See you then.'

Jay dialled again.

'BEEEP . . . Hello, this is 352 4591. I'm afraid I'm not able to come to the phone at the moment. But if you leave your name and number after the tone, I'll get back to you as soon as I can . . .'

'Carrie, this is Jay. I'm returning your message. The message you left after my last message. I'm going out soon, so if you call, you may find I'm not here.' He sighed. 'But if you want, you can leave a message on my machine . . .'

Outside the tall windows with their grey designer blinds, the sun was beginning to sink towards the horizon. Jay kicked off his shoes and walked over to the slim, black box that sat on the floor next to the skirting board. He slid a compact disc into it and went into the bathroom, where two auxiliary speakers were pumping out the music.

'I wanna be a sex monkey . . . swinging through the urban jungle . . .'

Jay jumped under the shower, closing his eyes and bellowing loudly. 'Sex monkey!' He lathered his body with Kudos cologne-scented deodorising sports shower gel, then stepped into the bedroom and began to climb into his clothes. Tasteful boxer shorts in a dark paisley print, Levis, a polo shirt and loafers without socks.

Outside, there was a parking ticket waiting on the wind-screen of the Twin-Cam Intercooler Turbo. Jay snatched it and crumpled it up in disgust. Then he spied a statuette of a cherub in a neighbour's garden, posing coyly behind a privet hedge. He stuffed the parking ticket into the cherub's hand.

'Serves them right for having something so naf,' he said out loud.

The electronic ignition fired, the twin carburettors roared, the quadrophonic in-car stereo system burst into song. Jay still hadn't decided how he was going to spend the evening, but he was unperturbed. He checked his Rolex. The night was still young.

At the same time, some fifty miles away in Cambridge, Leofred Plunkett was having the last tutorial of the summer.

It was the ninth week of term, and as soon as this tortuous hour was ended, the students would all be free to escape the cloistered world of the university for three and a half months. Leofred closed his eyes and listened to the clock on the mantelpiece, imagining its hands moving round the face. He played a game with himself. He would try and guess how far the minute hand had moved before he opened his eyes and checked the time. The idea was to try and keep from looking for as long as possible, so that more time would have passed. He opened his left eyelid cautiously. Twenty to seven. Twenty minutes still to go.

Leofred and his tutorial partner, Dave Jelling, were imprisoned in a dark, gloomy room in the mediaeval recesses of St Godbore's College. It was the study of their tutor, Peter Wimley, a room of which the owner was rather proud. Proud of its air of aesthetic squalor: the scrubby carpet that didn't quite meet the walls; the books piled haphazardly on every surface, including the floor, with their provocative titles, *The Superficies of Synonym, Questing for Id.* All had the air of having been read, or at least dipped into. Wimley sometimes spent whole evenings dreamily flexing their spines and dropping tell-tale coffee stains on their dust jackets. His own book, *Structuralism: a raison d'être,* lay face up in a prominent position.

Peter Wimley groped for the whisky decanter on his desk and poured himself a glass. He did not offer any to his pupils. He narrowed his eyes over the edge of the glass, allowing his shoulders to droop and burying his free hand deep in the pocket of his baggy cardigan. His were the mannerisms of an old man; the hesitant tread, the querulous voice. In fact he was thirty-nine.

Dave Jelling had just finished reading out his essay, punctuated by a lot of 'ums' and 'ers' and 'you sees'. He was wearing a T-shirt emblazoned with *'SEX AID – I screwed the world'*, and lime green track shoes.

Clearing his throat in order to read his own essay, Leofred wished he could be a bit more like the Dave Jellings of this world. That nonchalant scruffiness, that effortless appearance of having made no effort. Whatever he did, Leofred always managed to look neat and boring. His sweaters fitted him. His shoes remained unscuffed. Average height, average build. Average intelligence.

He gave a final cough and began.

'*The Wakefield Mystery Cycles.* The Wakefield Mystery Cycles have often been compared with the cycle of life itself. Indeed, it was the critic J. S. Threlfall who first made this comparison in 1903 when he wrote "*The Wakefield Mystery Cycles*, those monuments to the mystery of pro-creation . . ."'

Peter Wimley poured himself another glass of scotch with an ostentatiously windy sigh. Dave Jelling closed his eyes and leaned back in his chair. Leofred saw his hand move surreptitiously to his hip and switch on his Sony Walkman. Only ten minutes to go. He persevered, trying not to look at the clock.

'. . . and therefore in conclusion, we conclude that – '

'*We?*' snarled Peter Wimley. 'Who are "we"? To whom are you referring, for Christ's sake? Are you of royal blood?'

'No.' Leofred blinked.

'Well, content yourself with the first person singular then.'

Leofred opened his mouth to go on.

'No, no, we've had enough of that crap, thank you. I think I can guess what you were going to say. Have you actually *read The Wakefield Mystery Cycles*?'

'Yes.'

'Good God, most people don't bother,' Wimley finished his scotch and looked back at the clock. 'Well, gentlemen, I think we should devote the final five minutes to the usual summing up of the year's work. Mr Jelling . . .'

Dave Jelling was still plugged into his Walkman. He smiled benignly and went on tapping his foot.

'Mr Jelling . . . your essays have improved but they still read like political tracts for the left. There is no shred of literary appreciation in them anywhere. Go away and read some books.'

Dave Jelling continued to nod and tap his lime green shoe, like a fluorescent slug.

Wimley gave another of his exaggerated sighs and turned to Leofred. 'As for you, Mr Plunkett, I find you dull-witted in the extreme. Not an original thought, not an original idea has ever crossed your synapses. I suggest that your only hope is to – as you young people would put it – liven up your act a bit. You could either go away and transform yourself into a brilliant scholar, which I see as highly unlikely, or you could spend this summer doing something exciting, in the hope of emerging from your mediocrity.'

Leofred emerged, blinking, into the quadrangle of St Godbore's. The college was built in square formation around it, penetrated at intervals by numerous narrow doorways, like entrances to a rabbit warren. Through these doorways swarmed laughing, shouting students. They overflowed onto the large patch of grass in the middle of the quadrangle and draped themselves over the stone sundial at its centre. There were several girls amongst their number. St Godbore's prided itself on being one of the first male colleges to admit women, and although they did not yet